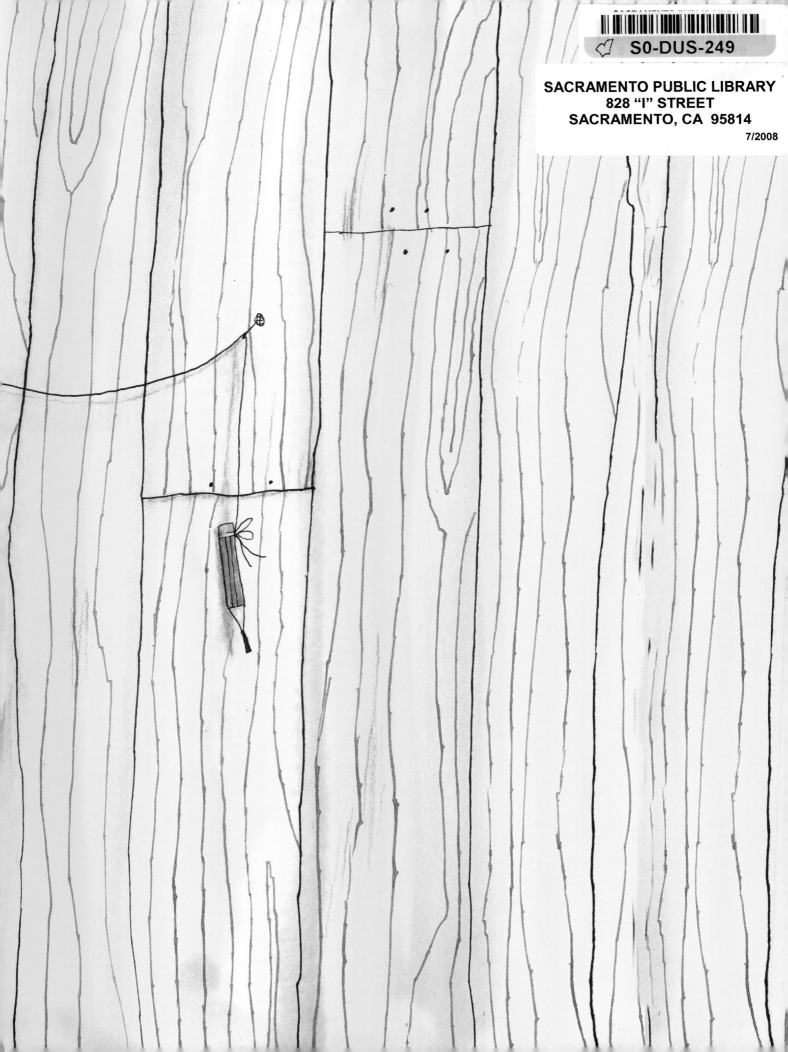

Copyright © 2007 by De Vier Windstreken, Netherlands.
First published in the Netherlands under the title *De Stem van Bever*.
English translation copyright © 2008 by North-South Books Inc., New York.

First published in the United States, Great Britain, Canada, Australia, and New Zealand in
2008 by North-South Books Inc., an imprint of NordSüd Verlag AG, Zürich, Switzerland.
Distributed in the United States by North-South Books Inc., New York.

Library of Congress Cataloging-in-Publication Data is available.
A CIP catalogue record for this book is available from The British Library.

ISBN: 978-0-7358-2195-8 (trade edition)
10 9 8 7 6 5 4 3 2 1

Printed in Belgium
www.northsouth.com

Henna Goudzand Nahar

A New Home for Beaver

Illustrated by Jeska Verstegen

NORTHSOUTH
BOOKS

New York / London

ONE DAY, while they were drinking their tea, Pig and Elephant heard someone singing.

"What a lovely, sweet voice," Pig sighed. "Who could that be?"

"I think we should investigate!" Elephant said as he straightened his tie.

As they reached the bend in the river they discovered Beaver, who was singing as he put a roof on his new house.

"Ahem!" said Elephant as he straightened his tie again.
Beaver looked down and saw Elephant and Pig standing there.
"Hello!" he shouted cheerfully as he climbed down the ladder.
"My dear sir," said Elephant. "May I ask what you are doing?"

"Well, the river where I was living dried up," Beaver replied.

"And?" Elephant asked impatiently.

"So now," answered Beaver, "I'm building a new home on the bank of this beautiful river."

"But you can't do that!" Elephant said, fiddling with his tie.
"Pig and I already live on the bank of this river."
"And *you* don't belong here!" Pig added.
"Why don't I belong here?" Beaver asked.
"Because," said Elephant, "we don't know you!"

"You're right!" said Beaver, hitting himself on the forehead. "Let me introduce myself. I am Beaver." Beaver smiled as he shook hands with Elephant and Pig.

"I am Elephant," replied Elephant.

"And I am Pig," said Pig.

Beaver started to climb up the ladder again to finish his roof, but Elephant stopped him.

"Excuse me, Beaver," said Elephant, "but just because we know your name doesn't mean you can live here!"

Beaver looked puzzled.

"We know nothing about you," explained Elephant.

"You're a stranger," added Pig.

"An intruder," Elephant said firmly.

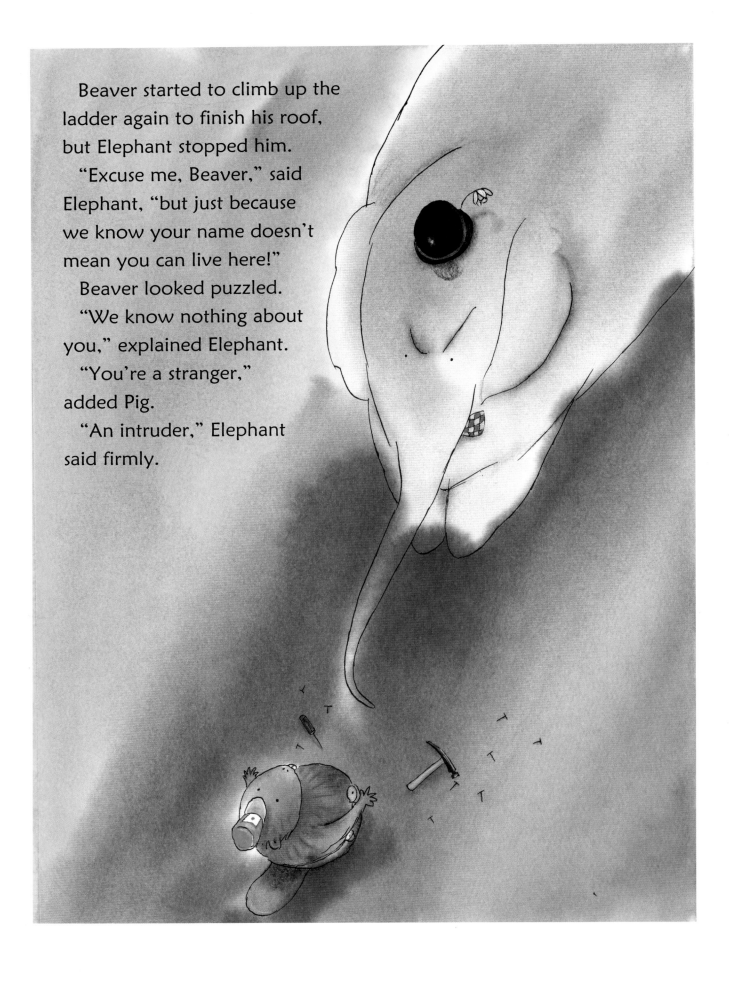

Beaver felt a little dizzy. Stranger, intruder; he had never been called these names before.

"Pig, Elephant," Beaver said, wiping a little sweat off his forehead, "do *you* have other names as well?"

"No, Beaver," Elephant replied. "Stranger and intruder, those are names for you."

"Names for someone who isn't welcome here," Pig added.

"And someone who isn't welcome here," said Elephant, "cannot live on this river bank."

"Well then," Beaver said, "please give me a name that *will* make me welcome here!"

"Dear Beaver," Elephant replied, "either you're welcome here or you're not."

"That's right!" said Pig.

"Do you want me to leave?" asked Beaver.

"Yes, you should leave," said Elephant as he straightened his tie yet again.

Beaver turned, picking up his backpack, and left. Just like that.

Elephant and Pig watched until they couldn't see Beaver anymore.
Then they walked home again.

Soon, Pig started to feel odd.

His eyes started to sting and his throat felt a little scratchy.

Pig looked at Elephant.

He saw Elephant's lower lip was trembling.

"Elephant," said Pig, "do you miss Beaver?"

Elephant straightened his tie once more.

"Saying goodbye is always difficult," he said. "Once we've had a good night's sleep, I'm sure we'll have forgotten all about Beaver."

And so, although it was only noon,
Elephant and Pig went straight
to bed.

The next morning when Pig woke up, he ran straight to Beaver's house.
Elephant did exactly the same.

"I don't understand," said Pig. "We had a good night's sleep, but Beaver is still on our minds."

"Perhaps we should have torn down Beaver's house. Once his house is gone, I'm sure we'll never think of him again," Elephant replied.

Elephant gave Pig a hammer.

Together they leveled Beaver's house completely.

"There, that's that!" said Elephant, wiping the dust off his clothes.

But Pig was still thinking of Beaver. He asked Elephant if he had already forgotten about him.

"It doesn't work that fast," Elephant replied. "Not for you, or for me. We'll have to get a good night's sleep before we forget Beaver completely."

And so, although it was only midday, Elephant and Pig went straight to bed again.

At dawn, Pig got up and ran to the place where Beaver's house had been. Elephant followed him.

"I just can't forget Beaver," Pig said sadly.

Elephant tried desperately to straighten his tie.

"Perhaps we acted a little hastily when we asked him to leave," Elephant admitted.

Pig walked over the rubble that used to be Beaver's house.

"Elephant, we have to get Beaver back!"

So Elephant and Pig followed the path that Beaver had taken the previous day.

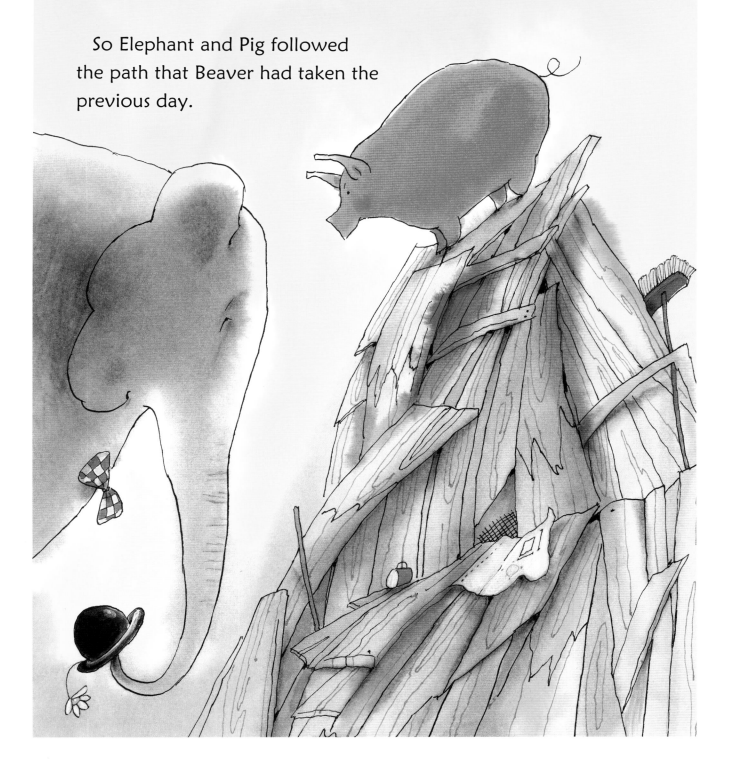

As they reached the middle of the forest, they heard someone singing.

"Beaver!" Elephant and Pig cried out together.

"Pig, Elephant, why have you come here?" Beaver whispered as he covered his face with his hands. "I was just trying to forget you."

"We tried to forget you, too," said Pig, "but we can't."

"And therefore," said Elephant importantly, finally managing to straighten his tie, "we would like to ask you to come back and live with us."

Pig and Elephant and Beaver walked together, back to the beautiful river.

And, together, they built a new house for Beaver.

And now, when Beaver sings his sweet song, Elephant and Pig say to each other, "Listen, that's the voice of our friend, Beaver!"